www.mascotbooks.com

SKIN-VINCIBLE: A STORY OF A SUPERSTAR WITH ICHTHYOSIS

For more information, please contact:
Mascot Kids, an imprint of Amplify Publishing Group
620 Herndon Parkway, Suite 320
Herndon, VA 20170
info@mascotbooks.com

Second printing. This Mascot Kids edition printed in 2023.

Library of Congress Control Number: 2022907357

CPSIA Code: PRKF0423B
ISBN-13: 978-1-63755-357-2

Printed in China

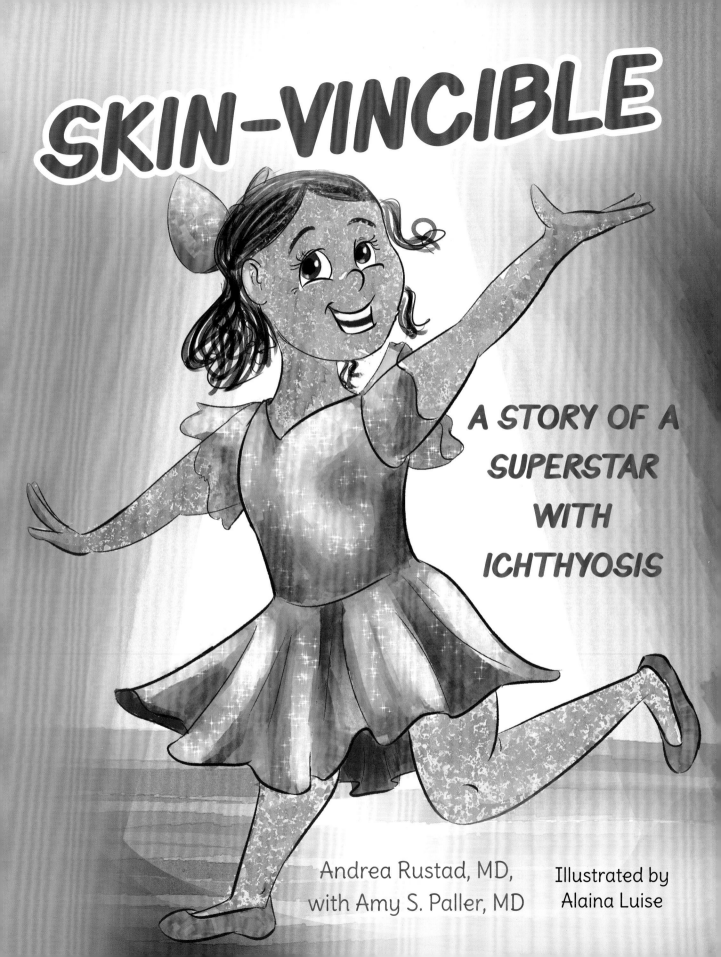

SKIN-VINCIBLE

A STORY OF A SUPERSTAR WITH ICHTHYOSIS

Andrea Rustad, MD,
with Amy S. Paller, MD

Illustrated by
Alaina Luise

Hi, my name is Cece, and today is my big day! I am singing and dancing in my school's talent show tonight! I am so excited, but also a little nervous. I have been practicing a lot. I can't wait to wear my sparkly, purple costume!

But first, I have to get up and take care of my skin because I have ichthyosis. It's pronounced *ICK—THEE—OH—SIS*. It's not a sunburn or just dry skin. I was born with ichthyosis and will always have it.

Some people with ichthyosis have a parent, sister, brother, or another family member with ichthyosis. But some kids—like me—are the only one in the family, and the only one they know with ichthyosis.

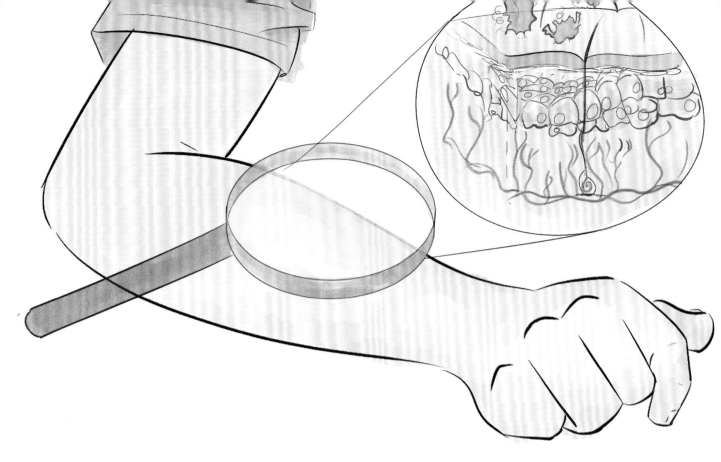

Did you know the skin is the largest organ in your body? Skin is like a wall that keeps water in and keeps germs out.

Skin is also like a layer cake with frosting between each outer layer of skin that makes the wall strong!

In ichthyosis, the skin doesn't work right. My skin grows super fast and piles up—like a very messy cake, which makes my skin extra dry and thick. It cracks easily, which can be painful.

I am **REALLY** itchy all the time, especially at night.

Not many people have my skin condition, but I have met others with ichthyosis at special camps or get-togethers. It's nice to know I am not alone with my skin. My friends with ichthyosis and I play games and talk just like any other kids.

Right now, ichthyosis is something I will have my whole life. But doctors and scientists are working hard to find a cure.

I've learned that there are **DOZENS** of kinds of ichthyosis because there are lots of ways the skin can be different.

People all over the world and with any skin color can have ichthyosis.

Some have dry, flaky, and bright red skin.

Others have really thick skin that's all piled up like mine.

It takes me a lot of time every day to take care of my skin. My parents help me too.

I take long baths, scrub off my extra skin, and then slather on creams. Extra skin can plug my ears. I have to get them cleaned out so I can hear.

Some of my friends with other kinds of ichthyosis have really tight skin around their eyes and can't even close them at night. They have to put in special eye drops.

Every person with ichthyosis has a different routine, because everyone's skin is unique. My doctors and my caregivers help me figure out what works for **ME** to keep my skin healthy.

When my skin is moisturized and happy, it makes me feel better and protects against germs. I am more comfortable to play and do the things I love!

Now that my skin is clean and moisturized, I am off to school!

I like school—my favorite class is science! I like doing fun experiments and learning about the world.

But my skin gets so dry and uncomfortable during the school day. I have to take breaks to put cream on, which my teacher reminds me to do.

My friends and I love recess, but I have to be extra careful. When it's hot, I can't be outside as long as others. I can't sweat so I easily overheat. I get even more itchy and tired. I have to make sure I keep cool, especially when I'm playing sports and games.

The thick skin on my feet can crack and hurt. That makes it hard for me to jump, run, and play. But if I take good care of my skin, I can still play along!

Even though our skin is different and takes extra work, kids with ichthyosis can still have fun outdoors and do normal activities.

I have fun with my friends at school. But for kids with ichthyosis like me, meeting new people can be tough. Some are scared of me and don't want to be near or touch me. Some people are just curious. Some stare or look away. Others are mean to me—they point at me, whisper, or even call me names.

Bullying, staring, or being left out of activities makes me sad and mad. I know that these feelings are normal, but getting angry doesn't help. I've had to learn how to stand up for myself, which isn't easy. I know that people usually aren't trying to be rude—they just don't understand. Telling people about ichthyosis, and that I can't spread it to others, helps people understand.

If you are being bullied, you can and should tell your parents, teachers, friends, or others you trust. You don't have to deal with it alone, and you should know that it isn't your fault.

If people don't accept you for who you are, they're not worth having as a friend. I can't change the way my skin looks. Good friends look past my skin and look at my fun personality.

My friends stick up for me and help me feel better if I am sad. It's important to have good friends and to be a good friend.

Finding something I love and am good at, like singing and dancing, helps me be more confident. I started dancing when I was just four years old. At first, it was scary to be on stage in front of so many people. But when I was dancing and having fun, I wasn't so bothered.

My friends also help me feel more comfortable with dancing on stage. They are coming to the talent show tonight to cheer me on. They really care about me!

Now it's my big moment! I take a deep breath and step onstage. I'm nervous, but I see the faces of my friends and family smiling from the audience. I smile back and know they believe in me. The music starts and I sing along, twirling and jumping. I have so much fun!

When I finish, I curtsy and the whole room claps. I feel like a star!

Remember, my skin is only one part of who I am. It's just my outside, like **WRAPPING PAPER!**

The real **GIFTS** we all have are inside of ourselves. I have a fun personality and many talents. I care about my family and friends. I like playing games and learning new things—just like other kids.

If you have ichthyosis like I do, don't be ashamed! It makes you special. Ichthyosis isn't contagious, but your confidence can be.

If you are comfortable with yourself, others will like you for who you are and be comfortable around you too. Don't be afraid to try new things—even dancing on stage—and try not to worry about what others think of you.

Everyone has differences. Some are just more visible than others. If you see someone who looks different, don't stare, tease, or leave them out. Say hi and get to know them!

We are all different, but we can be friends and help each other. And together we can be **SKIN-VINCIBLE!**

THE END

ABOUT THE AUTHORS

ANDREA RUSTAD, MD

Andrea Rustad graduated with her MD in 2023 from the Northwestern University Feinberg School of Medicine in Chicago, Illinois, and hopes to specialize in pediatric dermatology. Dr. Rustad has atopic dermatitis, taking extra time and care for her skin since childhood. Her condition blossomed into an interest in dermatology. She first met children with ichthyosis as a counselor at Camp Discovery, a camp for children with skin conditions, which motivated her to learn more about ichthyosis and get involved in ichthyosis research with Dr. Paller. Dr. Rustad wrote short stories as a child and has always loved reading and writing. *Skin-vincible* is her first book.

AMY S. PALLER, MD

Amy S. Paller, MD, is a pediatric dermatologist who specializes in genetic skin disorders, including ichthyosis. She is the Walter J. Hamlin Professor and Chair of the Department of Dermatology and Professor of Pediatrics at the Northwestern University Feinberg School of Medicine, where she also directs the Skin Disease Research Center. She has written almost 600 articles, including many related to ichthyosis, is the author of leading textbooks on dermatology, and has led several clinical trials to find new treatments for ichthyosis. Dr. Paller has served on the Medical and Scientific Advisory Board of FIRST for more than twenty-five years and is currently an emeritus member of its board of directors.

After hearing from many children and families about the lack of media representation and public knowledge of ichthyosis, Dr. Paller and Dr. Rustad thought that a children's book on ichthyosis could be both enjoyable and helpful; this idea was met with enthusiasm from the ichthyosis community.

MEET SOME OTHER SUPERSTARS WITH ICHTHYOSIS!

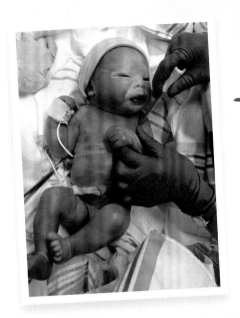 →

Here is an awareness card from the Foundation for Ichthyosis and Related Skin Types (FIRST) that you can cut out to hand to people that explains your/your child's condition! Here is a website where you can order more:

FIRSTSKINFOUNDATION.ORG/AWARENESS-CARD

Hi! I was born with a rare skin disorder called **ichthyosis**.
My skin works differently because of a genetic mutation I was born with.
It is just one part of who I am.

Ichthyosis is not contagious. I don't have a bad sunburn or poor bathing habits.
I want to educate people so others like me don't experience stares, teasing, or rudeness.

For more info about **ichthyosis** or to support research to find a cure, contact the
Foundation for Ichthyosis and Related Skin Types
at: 800-545-3286
www.FIRSTskinfoundation.org

Different is beautiful.

first
Foundation for Ichthyosis & Related Skin Types